The Witchling's Wish

For Ann & Iain – the kindest people I know,

love L.F. xxx

For Aria, Ella, Leia and Loretta
– S.M.

BLOOMSBURY CHILDREN'S BOOKS
Bloomsbury Publishing Plc
50 Bedford Square, London, WC1B 3DP, UK
29 Earlsfort Terrace, Dublin 2, Ireland

BLOOMSBURY, BLOOMSBURY CHILDREN'S BOOKS and the Diana logo
are trademarks of Bloomsbury Publishing Plc
First published in Great Britain 2021 by Bloomsbury Publishing Plc
This edition published 2022

Text copyright © Sarah Maclean 2021
Illustrations copyright © Sarah Massini 2021

Sarah Maclean and Sarah Massini have asserted their rights under the Copyright,
Designs and Patents Act, 1988, to be identified as Author and Illustrator of this work

A catalogue record for this book is available from the British Library

ISBN 978 1 4088 9996 0 (PB)
ISBN 978 1 4088 9995 3 (HB)
ISBN 978 1 4088 9994 6 (eBook)

1 3 5 7 9 10 8 6 4 2

Printed and bound in China by C&C Offset Printing Co Ltd,
Shenzhen, Guangdong

To find out more about our authors and books visit
www.bloomsbury.com
and sign up for our newsletters

Lu Fraser

The
Witchling's
Wish

Illustrated by

Sarah Massini

BLOOMSBURY
CHILDREN'S BOOKS
LONDON OXFORD NEW YORK NEW DELHI SYDNEY

Above the misty mountains,
below a glowing moon,
lived a lonely little Witchling
with a wobbly, knobbly broom . . .

And a squeaky, leaky cauldron,
and a not-so-pointy hat,
and a spell book full of spellings,
in a cave of inky bats.

Now, the Little Witchling
didn't mind
the beetles in her bed,

and she didn't mind

the drip,

drip,

drip

of water on her head.

But deep inside
her Witchling heart
there was
an empty space,

"I wish I had a **friend**," she sighed,
"to fill this lonely place."

"I can't **grow** one!
I can't **sew** one! Hmmm . . ."
The Witchling scratched her head,
"I know!" she cried,
"I'll cast a spell . . .

and **MAGIC** one instead!"

So she opened up her spell book
and she checked her shopping list,

for all the things she'd need to weave
a friendship-making wish . . .

"A cup or two of cobwebs, some earwax from a lizard . . .

a pirate's boot,

a blue owl's hoot

and snowflakes from a blizzard."

"At last," the Little Witchling hummed,
"my spell is almost ready!
All that's missing is some furriness from . . . Oh!

A *One-Eyed* TEDDY?"

"A TEDDY?" frowned the Witchling.

"I bet it's huge and hairy!
With spiky claws and gnashing jaws –
it sounds EXTREMELY scary!"

"But if I want my wish to work,
I'll HAVE to face this TED . . .

And there's one at 14 Acorn Drive, my crystal ball has said!"

So off she WHOOSHED into the night, aboard her wobbly broom,

and when the house loomed into sight . . .

She peered into a room.
BUT . . .

The curtains twitched!

Her broomstick pitched!

She flew
heels over head!

And

landed

by

a

little

girl

and on a ONE-EYED TED!

"I'm Lily," said the little girl,
"it's very nice to meet you!"

"STAND BACK!" the Witchling cried in fear,

"THAT One-Eyed TED might EAT you!"

"My Ted," said Lily firmly,
"is **not** the eating kind!
He may look a little different,
but that's **NOT** a thing I mind.

And though I've hugged off
all his fur

and one ear hangs in tatters,

he's been my FRIEND forever . . .

and to me,
that's ALL that matters."

"You've hugged off **all** his furriness?"
the Little Witchling cried.
"My **wishing spell** will **NOT** go well
without **Ted's fur!**" she sighed.

"You see, I'd hoped to magic up a **friend,**"
the Witchling said.
And her not-so-pointy Witchling hat
drooped **sadly** on her head.

"Well . . ." said Lily, thoughtfully,
"there is just **ONE** last hair.
And if you really need it . . .
then Ted and I will **SHARE!**"

"You'd give," the Witchling said, amazed,
"your Ted's last hair to ME?
Well, I think **your heart** is bigger
than I thought a heart could be!"

But she saw how Lily LOVED her bear,
and then the Witchling knew
that taking One-Eyed Ted's last hair
she simply couldn't do!

And sighing just a little,
the Witchling turned away,
but Lily and her One-Eyed Ted
jumped up and called out . . .

"STAY!"

"Don't you see?" laughed Lily,
"That's what a **friend** would do!
You thought of **me**, you thought of **Ted**,
you *didn't* think of . . . YOU!"

Then Lily **hugged** the Witchling,
and they both hugged One-Eyed Ted.

"Your Witchling heart is BIG enough
for ALL of us!" she said.

And that was how,
through **kindness**,
the Witchling made a **friend**
and though her spell was never cast,
her **wish** worked in . . .

. . . The End.